PROFESSOR FERGUS FAHRENHEIT

AND

HIS

WONDERFUL WEATHER MACHINE

For my parents, Charles and Carol Groth
—C.G.F.

To Anna, Nancy, Julie and Kathy
—D.W.

PROFESSOR FERGUS FAHRENHEIT

AND HIS

WONDERFUL WEATHER MACHINE

BY CANDACE GROTH-FLEMING

ILLUSTRATED BY DON WELLER

SIMON & SCHUSTER BOOKS FOR YOUNG READERS
Published by Simon & Schuster
New York London Toronto Sydney Tokyo Singapore

Dry Gulch, Texas, was as dry as last year's
fallen leaves. Hot winds swept across the flat
plains, bending the thirsty trees and raising
the parched soil into clouds of swirling dust.

The citizens of Dry Gulch watched their crops wither and die. They scanned the cloudless sky for signs of rain. They worried. They prayed. And finally, they called a town meeting.

The townsfolk gathered at the Old Reliable Dry Goods Store, squeezed in between bolts of calico and boxes of nails, between bags of sugar and barrels of flour. All eyes turned toward Dry Gulch's mayor.

Mayor McHugh stood. He puffed out his cheeks, cleared his dry throat, and declared, "People of Dry Gulch, we have a terrible problem. We have had no rain in weeks, and there's no sign that any is on the way. Without rain our crops cannot live, and without our crops *we* cannot live. We must find a solution to this problem—and soon!"

The townsfolk nodded and muttered their agreement. Then they sat quietly, waiting to hear what the mayor had to suggest. But their silence was met with silence, because Mayor McHugh had absolutely no ideas to offer.

Suddenly, the bell over the store's front door tinkled, and in walked the strangest figure the people of Dry Gulch had ever seen. He was dressed in black from the tips of his dusty shoes to the top of his plug hat. In one hand he carried an odd red gripsack.

"Good afternoon, ladies and gentlemen," the stranger said, bowing at the waist and tipping his hat. "My name is Professor Fergus Fahrenheit, and I represent the Wonder-Worker Weather Company. I understand you folks are in need of some rain. Well, ours is of the very best quality; and with every order we throw in a free silk umbrella."

Professor Fahrenheit pulled an order pad and a stubby pencil from his vest pocket. "What will it be, folks?" he asked. "A fine drizzle? A soaking summer shower? Or a real ear-banger of a thunderstorm?"

Mayor McHugh puffed out his cheeks even farther, his face turning an angry red. "Your claim that you can make rain is just so much *more* hot air, Professor What's-Your-Name," he shouted. "Now get out of here, and let us get back to solving our problem."

"But my dear mayor," replied the professor, "*I'm* here to solve your problem. By using the Wonder-Worker Weather Machine, I can make this dusty plain blossom like a rose."

"Poppycock," snorted the mayor.

"Fact," insisted the professor. "But I can see that none of you believes me, so I'll just have to give you a sample shower. Free of charge, of course."

Before the mayor could say another word, Fahrenheit hurried outside. There was nothing for the townsfolk to do but follow him.

In the center of Main Street, the professor opened wide his mysterious gripsack, and out came a wondrous cornucopia of hardware.

There were batteries and glass bottles, copper wires and metal coils, tin funnels, test tubes, and more. Professor Fahrenheit snapped the hodgepodge of pieces together and reached into his bag once more. Out came a long, thin pipe and a large crank. He attached the pipe to the top of the contraption and stuck the crank in its side.

"Now here we go, my friends," said the professor, and he began to turn the crank.

Black smoke puffed from the pipe atop the contraption, and a smell like rotten eggs filled the air. A whirring, fluttering sound like the buzzing of an enormous bee floated on the sudden breeze.

A great sigh of wonder escaped from the residents of Dry Gulch as a cool mist of rain swirled around them, tickling their faces and freckling the dusty street. The townsfolk laughed with pleasure and clapped one another on the back, as children took off their shoes and socks and pranced through the little puddles that began to form.

"Do you believe me now?" Professor Fahrenheit called out to the mayor.

"Coincidence," answered the mayor, "nothing but coincidence."

"I take it you need more proof, then," said Fahrenheit, and he began to crank his weather machine a bit faster.

Black clouds appeared and raced across the sky. Thunder rumbled and lightning flashed. Instead of the gentle drizzle of a few minutes before, a heavy rain poured down, turning the streets to mud and stinging the faces of the amazed townsfolk, who dashed for cover under the awning of the dry goods store.

"Well, Mr. Mayor, do you need any more proof?" asked Professor Fahrenheit.

"I still say you're a fraud," replied the stubborn mayor, now soaked to the skin.

"Well, perhaps this will convince you," said the professor as he cranked his machine even faster.

The day turned to darkness, and a storm like no one could remember roared into town. Buildings rattled. Windows shook. Roof tiles, mailboxes, street signs, and chickens were picked up by the wind and swirled through the air. Main Street quickly became a river, and the townsfolk held on for dear life to whatever was handy so they wouldn't be swept away.

"Need more convincing, Your Honor?" Professor Fahrenheit shouted at the mayor so he could be heard above the wind and rain.

Before the mayor could speak, a cry rose up from Dry Gulch's soggy citizens.

"No more convincing," they pleaded.

"We believe you," they hollered.

"You have our business," they promised.

And then, before you could say *"Rain, rain, go away,"* that's just what happened; and the sun came out to boot.

Out of his pocket Professor Fahrenheit again took his order pad and pencil.

"Well, my friends," he asked, "what will it be? A bit more rain?"

"No!" came the shout from the chorus of townsfolk.

"Then how about some sleet, or snow, or hail?" asked the professor.

"Please, no!" came the answer.

"Well, then," said Professor Fahrenheit, "why don't I just write up an order for a summer of sunshine, with just enough rain to keep your crops growing, your gardens flowering, and the little ones happy with their puddle jumping?"

"Yes!" they all cried, and proceeded to make a deal with the professor that made everyone happy.

"I'll be off, then," said Fergus Fahrenheit as he took apart his amazing contraption and packed it away in his gripsack, "but I'll be back next summer."

And so he was, and every summer afterward.
The folks of Dry Gulch were always happy to
see him return, always signed on the dotted
line for his services, and never again asked for
a sample demonstration of his wonderful
weather machine.

Author's Note

Between 1880 and 1930, "professional" rainmakers cropped up like weeds every spring to make a profit out of hard luck. Their appearance in drought-stricken states like Kansas, Nebraska, the Dakotas, Texas, even California was common, and more often than not, desperate townspeople joined together to buy "artificially made rain."

Each rainmaker had his own approach to making rain, but the favorite method was through the use of scientific-looking contraptions with mysterious chemicals and crank handles. Professor Fahrenheit's weather machine is modeled on the rainmaking device of Frank Melbourne, a famous rainmaker who worked in Kansas.

Professor Fahrenheit himself is a composite of several real rainmakers. His offer to "throw in a silk umbrella with every order" came from the salespitch of a rainmaker working for the Aquarius Rainmaking Company of Goodland, Kansas. Fahrenheit's physical appearance is actually a description of rainmaker Ambrosius Sykes of Texas. And Fahrenheit's "sample shower" was taken from an account of Frank Melbourne's exploits.

An actual incident that occured in California, however, was the basis for this book. According to first-hand accounts, in January of 1917 the city of San Diego paid rainmaker Charles Hatfield thousands of dollars to end their drought. And end it he did! He brought forth the biggest rainfall the area had ever seen, which eventually lead to the biggest flood the area had ever had. Even though we know that rainmaking is impossible, the people of San Diego were convinced that the flood was Hatfield's fault. They called the disaster "Hatfield's Flood," and actually tried to sue the rainmaker for damages. Their suit didn't hold water, but it makes a great story.

SIMON & SCHUSTER BOOKS FOR YOUNG READERS 1230 Avenue of the Americas, New York, New York 10020. Text copyright © 1994 by Candace Groth-Fleming. Illustrations copyright © 1994 by Don Weller. All rights reserved including the right of reproduction in whole or in part in any form. SIMON & SCHUSTER BOOKS FOR YOUNG READERS is a trademark of Simon & Schuster. The text for this book is set in 14 point Goudy. The illustrations were done in watercolor. Manufactured in the United States of America 10 9 8 7 6 5 4 3 2 1
Library of Congress Cataloging-in-Publication Data Groth-Fleming, Candace. Professor Fergus Fahrenheit and his wonderful weather machine/ by Candace Groth-Fleming; illustrated by Don Weller. p. cm. Summary: When the inhabitants of Dry Gulch wonder if they will survive the terrible drought that afflicts their town, Professor Fahrenheit offers to bring them rain with his amazing weather machine. [1. Droughts—Fiction. 2. Rain and rainfall—Fiction. 3. Inventions—Fiction.] I. Weller, Don, ill. II. Title. PZ7.F59936Pr 1994 [E]—dc20 93-4432 CIP ISBN: 0-671-87047-5